Edward Sandford Martin

Sly Ballades in Harvard China

Edward Sandford Martin

Sly Ballades in Harvard China

ISBN/EAN: 9783743334656

Manufactured in Europe, USA, Canada, Australia, Japa

Cover: Foto ©Andreas Hilbeck / pixelio.de

Manufactured and distributed by brebook publishing software
(www.brebook.com)

Edward Sandford Martin

Sly Ballades in Harvard China

SLY BALLADES IN HARVARD CHINA

By E. S. M

BOSTON
A. WILLIAMS AND COMPANY
OLD CORNER BOOKSTORE
1882

CONTENTS.

MIXED.

WITHIN my earthly temple there 's a crowd:
There 's one of us that 's humble, one that 's proud;
There 's one that 's broken-hearted for his sins,
And one who, unrepentant, sits and grins;
There 's one who loves his neighbor as himself,
And one who cares for naught but fame and pelf.
From much corroding care I should be free
If once I could determine which is Me.

ONLY.

ONLY a small bit of paper,
With just a few dates, — nothing more, —
Which at an unfortunate moment
Glides down from my sleeve to the floor.

Only an Argus-eyed proctor,
Who, ever upon the *qui vive*,
Picks up, with suppressed exultation,
The paper which dropped from my sleeve.

Only four months in the country, —
An extra vacation, that 's all ;
But the trade of a proctor still strikes me
As something exceedingly small.

PROCUL NEGOTIIS.

I THINK that if I had a farm
I 'd be a man of sense;
And if the day was bright and warm
I 'd sit upon the fence,
And calmly smoke a pensive pipe,
And think about my pigs,
And wonder if the corn was ripe,
And counsel *l'homme qui* digs.

And if the day was wet and cold,
I think I should admire
To sit and dawdle over old
Montaigne, before the fire ;
And pity boobies who could lie
And squabble, just for pelf,
And thank my lucky stars that I
Was nicely fixed myself.

THE SONG OF THE BLOOD.

SOME like upon the winding Charles
To ply the bending oar ;
Nor reck they if their backs are burned
And every muscle sore.
But as for me, it suits me not :
I 'll ever be content
To loaf in front of Holworthy,
And toss the shining cent.

Some like to hurl the pig-skin sphere
Ofttimes on Jarvis field ;
Nor ask a greater pleasure than
The willow bat to wield.
But as for me, it suits me best,
With calm, unruffled mien,
To loaf in front of Holworthy,
And gamble on the green.

Some like to grind the livelong day,
And think it is immense
To study for their annuals,
And take in large per cents;
But as for me, oh, give me rest,
And let me, free from care,
Sit on the steps of Holworthy,
And take the evening air!

THE LOAFER'S LAMENT.

My heated brain is burning,
My soul for rest is yearning,
Speak to me not concerning
    My duties as a grind :
But bring the cooling tankard
For which I long have hankered :
When at my side it 's anchored
    I 'll consolation find.

Fair Idleness, thou devil !
Thou charming sprite of evil !
How in thy charms I 'll revel
    When my degree is won !
But if to-day I woo thee,
To-morrow I shall rue thee,
With longing eyes I view thee,
    While yet thy spells I shun.

JILTED.

Stay me with flagons, . . . for I am sick of love. — CANT. II. 5.

To seem gay and youthful I 'm trying,
But my heart is as old as the hills,
And I feel that those parties are lying
Who tell me that grief never kills.

My story has oft been related;
I fit in an old, old groove,
Since never, as some one has stated,
The course of true love ran smooth.

Susceptible, young, and romantic,
I thought her an angel of light;
And still, save when grief makes me frantic,
I firmly believe I was right.

An angel she was, but the healing
She bore on her wings was a part
Of the means that she used for annealing
Another young man's broken heart.

And that 's why I say, " Bring on flagons,
And place them convenient for me! "
'T is not that I wish to see dragons
And snakes, as we do in " D. T."

No, no : 't is because I would quiet
This sorrow to which I am linked ;
While fancy, unshackled, runs riot,
And memories grow indistinct.

Let me cherish once more the delusion
That girls are as true as they seem,
And, during my mental confusion,
Imagine it all was a dream.

BROKE, BROKE, BROKE!

Broke, broke, broke!
I have squandered the uttermost sou,
And have failed in my efforts to utter
One trivial, last I. O. U.

Oh, well for the infant in arms
That for ducats he need not fret;
Oh, well for the placid corpse
That he 's settled his final debt.

And dun after dun comes in,
Each bringing his little account;
And oh for the touch of a five-dollar bill,
Or a check for a large amount!

Broke, broke, broke!
My course as a student is run;
I 'll back to my childhood's home, and act
The rôle of the Prodigal Son.

REFORM.

Yes, I know that I once was a bummer,
The laziest drone of the swarm;
But I tell you I started last summer
The glorious work of reform.

As Freshman I swallowed my bitters,
And thought that I cut quite a dash;
A Soph'more I raised endless litters
Of pups, and a feeble mustache;

A Junior, — how oft the Dean's letter
Made the hearts of my parents feel sore!
I was young then, but now I know better, —
I 'll never do so any more.

2

Don't speak of the bliss of potation,
Don't tell me that lager is cheap :
Don't hint that I need recreation,
Nor doubt if I get enough sleep.

Ere I spend it I look at each nickel
With fond, parsimonious care;
P'r'aps you notice how Time's ruthless sickle
Has shortened the trousers I wear!

Am I thin? Quite correct your conjecture.
Memorial Hall is the place :
We breakfast upon architecture,
For luncheon we merely say grace.

While you, sir, are placidly sleeping
The sleep of the thoughtless and free,
A studious party is keeping
A vigil in my room : That's me.

I know that they were evanescent,
My many reforms of the past;
But I feel myself certain, at present,
That this one is going to last.

A GUM GAME.

How sweet, while lingering near a
    cross-walk muddy,
When Sol in March dissolves the tardy snows,
To lose one's self in contemplative study!
Of symmetry which gathered skirts disclose!

But how disheartening when, to optics eager
To glean of patient watchfulness the fruits,
The petticoat, soil scorning, grants a meagre
Display of dingy, shapeless rubber boots!

FUIT ILIUM.

WERE you nurtured in the purple?
Were you reared a 'pampered pet?
Did a menial throng encircle
You, in waiting while you ate?
When a baby, had you lockets,
Silver cups and forks and spoons?
Were there coins in the pockets
Of your childhood's pantaloons?

Did hereditary shekels
Make your sweethearts deem you fair, —
Reconcile them to your freckles
And your carrot-colored hair?
In electrifying raiment
Were you every day attired?
Was the promptness of your payment
Universally admired?

Did your father, too confiding,
Sign the paper of his friends?
Did his railway-stock, subsiding,
Cease to pay him dividends?
Are his buildings slow in renting?
Did his banker pilfer, slope,
And, absconding, leave lamenting
Creditors to live on hope?

.   .   .   .

Ere you dissipate a quarter
Do you scrutinize it twice?
Have you ceased to look on water
Drinking as a nauseous vice?
Do you wear your brother's breeches,
Though the buttons scarcely meet?
Does the vanity of riches
Form no part of your conceit?

I am with you, fellow pauper!
Let us share our scanty crust;

Burst the bonds of fiscal torpor,
Go where beer is sold on trust.
Let us, freed from *res angustæ,*
Seek some fair Utopian mead,
Where the throat is never dusty,
And tobacco grows — a weed.

EPITHALAMIUM.

HE marriage-bells have rung their
peal,
The wedding-march has told its story;
I 've seen her at the altar kneel
In all her stainless virgin glory;
She 's bound to honor, love, obey,
Come joy or sorrow, tears or laughter.
I watched her as she rode away,
And flung the lucky slipper after.

She was my first, my very first,
My earliest inamorata;
And to the passion that I nursed
For her I almost was a martyr.
For I was young, and she was fair,
And always bright and gay and chipper;
And oh, she wore such pretty hair!
Such silken stockings! Such a slipper!

She did not wish to make me mourn, —
She was the kindest of God's creatures;
But flirting was in her inborn,
Like brains and queerness in the Beechers.
I do not fear your heartless flirt, —
Obtuse her dart and dull her probe is;
But when girls do not mean to hurt,
But *do*, — *Orate tunc pro nobis!*

A most romantic country place;
The moon at full, the month of August;

An inland lake, across whose face
Played gentle zephyrs, ne'er a raw gust ;
Books, boats, and horses, to enjoy
The which was all our occupation,
A damsel and a callow boy ; —
There! Now you have the situation.

We rode together miles and miles ;
My pupil she, and I her Chiron.
At home I reveled in her smiles,
And read her extracts out of Byron.
We roamed by moonlight, chose our stars
(I thought it most authentic billing),
Explored the woods, climbed over bars,
Smoked cigarettes, and broke a shilling.

An infinitely blissful week
Went by in this Arcadian fashion :
I hesitated long to speak,
But ultimately breathed my passion.

She said her heart was not her own;
She said she 'd love me like a sister;
She cried a little (not alone);
I told her not to fret, and — kissed her.

I lost some sleep, some pounds in weight,
A deal of time, and all my spirits;
And much — how much I dare not state —
I mused upon that damsel's merits.
I tortured my unhappy soul;
I wished I never might recover;
I hoped her marriage-bells might toll
A requiem for her faithful lover.

And now she 's married; now she wears
A wedding-ring upon her finger:
And I — although it odd appears —
Still in the flesh I seem to linger.
Lo, there my swallow-tail, and here
Lies by my side a wedding favor;

Beside it stands a mug of beer;
I taste it, — how divine it 's flavor!

I saw her, in her bridal dress,
Stand pure and lovely at the altar;
I heard her firm response — that " Yes "
Without a quiver or a falter.
And here I sit and drink to her
Long life and happiness, God bless her!
Now fill again!   No heel-taps, sir!
Here 's to — success to her successor!

AGAIN.

I WONDER why my brow is burning,
Why sleep to close my lids forgets;
I wonder why I have a yearning
To smoke incessant cigarettes.
I wonder why my thoughts will wander,
And all restraint of mine defy,
And why — excuse the rhyme — a gander
Is not more of a goose than I.

I have an indistinct impression
I had these symptoms once before,
And dull discomfort held possession
Of the same spot that now is sore;
That some time, in a past that ranges
From early whiskers up to bibs,
My heart was ringing just such changes
As now, against these self-same ribs.

I wish some philanthropic Jenner
Might vaccinate against these ills,
And help us keep our noiseless tenor
Of life submissive to our wills;
And, ere our hearts were permeated
With sentiments too warm by half,
That we might be inoculated
With the mild passion of a calf.

SNOWBOUND.

A Law Office; two Briefless Ones; a Clock strikes.

JAMES.

ONE, two, three, four. It's four o'clock;
There comes the postman round the block,
And in a jiff we'll hear his knock
    Most pleasant.
Inform me, Thomas, will he bring
To you, deserving no such thing,
Letters from her whose praises ring
    Incessant ?

THOMAS.

Friend of my bosom, James, refrain
From putting questions fraught with pain,
And seeking facts I had not fain
    Imparted.

The said official on this stretch
Will not, in my opinion, fetch
Such documents to me, a wretch
    Down hearted.

JAMES.

Nay; but I prithee, Thomas, tell
To me, thy friend, who loves thee well,
What cause there is for such a fell
    Deprival.
Why is it that the message fails?
Have broken ties, or twisted rails,
Or storm, or snow delayed the mail's
    Arrival?

THOMAS.

Thou art, O James, a friend indeed
To probe my wound and make it bleed:
To know of my affairs thy greed
    Has no bound.

3

The reason why you have not guessed;
If storm there were, 't was in her breast;
For there my letter, unexpressed,
    Lies snowbound.

TO MABEL.

UPON this anniversar*ee*
My little god-child, aged three,
These compliments I make to thee,
    Quite heedless.
And that you'll throw them now away,
But treasure them some future day,
Are platitudes, the which to say
        Is needless.

You small, stout damsel, mickle mou'd,
With cropped tow-head and manners rude,
And stormy spirit unsubdued
     By nurses,
Where you were raised, was it in vogue
To lisp that Tipperary brogue?
Oh, you're a subject sweet, you rogue,
     For verses!

Last Sunday morning, when we stayed
At home, you got yourself arrayed
In Lyman's clothes, and turned from maid
     To urchin;
And when we all laughed at you so
You eyed outside the falling snow,
And thought your rig quite fit to go
     To church in.

Play on! play on, dear little lass!
Play on till sixteen summers pass,

And then I 'll bring a looking-glass,
  And there be-
Fore you, on your lips, I 'll show
The curves of small Dan Cupid's bow;
And then the crop that now is " tow "
  Shall "fair" be.

And then I 'll show you, too, the charms
Of small firm hands and rounded arms,
And eyes whose flashes send alarms
  Right through you ;
And then a half-regretful sigh
May break from me to think that I,
At forty years, can never try
  To woo you,

What shall I wish you ?　Free from ruth
To live and learn in love and truth
Through childhood's day and days of youth,
  And school's day ;

For all the days that intervene
Twixt Mab at three and at nineteen
Are but one sombre or serene
All Fool's Day.

MEA CULPA.

THERE is a thing, which, in my brain
Though nightly I revolve it,
I cannot in the least explain,
Nor do I hope to solve it.
While others tread the narrow path,
In manner meek and pious,
Why is it that my spirit hath
So opposite a bias?

Brought up to fear the Lord, and dread
The bottomless abysm,
In Watts's hymns profoundly read,
And drilled in catechism,
I should have been a model youth,
The pink of all that 's proper.
I was not; but, to tell the truth,
I did not care a copper.

I had no yearnings, when a boy,
To sport an angel's wrapper,
Nor heard I with tumultuous joy
The church-frequenting clapper.
My actions always harmonized
With my own sweet volition :
I always did what I devised,
But rarely asked permission.

When o'er the holy book I 'd pore,
And read of doings pristine,
I had a fellow-feeling for
The put-upon Philistine.
King David gratified my taste, —
He harped, and danced boleros ;
But first the Prodigal was placed
Upon my list of heroes.

I went to school. To study ? No !
I dearly loved to dally

And dawdle over Ivanhoe,
Tom Brown, and Charles O'Malley.
In recitation, I was used
To halt on every sentence ;
Repenting, seldom I produced
Fruits proper for repentance.

At college, later, I became
Familiar with my Flaccus ;
Brought incense to the Muses' flame,
And sacrificed to Bacchus.
I flourished in an air unfraught
With sanctity's aroma ;
Learned many things I was not taught,
And captured a diploma.

I am not well provided for,
I have no great possessions ;
I do not like the legal or
Medicinal professions.

Were I of good repute, I might
Take orders as a deacon ;
But I 'm no bright and shining light,
But just a warning beacon.

Though often urged by friends sincere
To woo some funded houri,
I cannot read my title clear
To any damsel's dowry.
And could to wedlock I induce
An heiress, I should falter,
For fear that such a bridal noose
Might prove a gilded halter.

My tradesmen have suspicious grown ;
My friends are tired of giving ;
Upon the cold, cold world I 'm thrown,
To hammer out my living.
I fear that work before me lies :
Indeed, I see no option,

Unless, perhaps, I advertise
" An orphan — for adoption ! "

A legacy of misspent time
Is all that I 'm the heir to ;
I cannot make my life sublime,
However much I care to.
And if, as now, I turn my head
In retrospect a minute,
'T is but to recognize my bed
Before I lie down in it.

I am the man that I have been,
And at the final summing
How shall I bear to see sent in
My score, — one long shortcoming!
Unless when all the saints exclaim,
With righteous wrath, " *Peccavit !* "
Some mighty friend shall make his claim,
" He suffered, and — *amavit !* "

A MORTIFYING SUBJECT.

WHAT is to be, I do not know;
What is, I do esteem
To be so undesirable
And worthless that I deem
There must be something good in store, —
Something to keep in view,
To reconcile us living here
For living as we do.

For life, — oh life, it seems a chore;
Its surface is so blurred
By storms of passion that it makes
One long to be interred;
To occupy a tranquil spot
Some seven feet by two,
And just serenely lie and rot,
With nothing else to do.

I think that when there ceased to be
Sufficient tenement
To hold my conscience, then I would
Begin to be content.
And if I should be there to see
My stomach take its leave,
I 'd gather up my mouldering shroud
And chuckle in my sleeve.

I think that when the greedy worm
Began upon my brains,
I 'd wish him luck, and hope he 'd get
His dinner for his pains.
I 'd warn him that they would be apt
With him to disagree,
For if they fed him well, 't were what
They seldom did for me.

But when I should be certain that
My scarred and battered heart

Was of my corporality
Not any more a part,
Though I 'd no voice, I 'd rattle in
My throat with joyous tones,
And, with no feelings left, I would
Feel happy in my bones.

IN THE ELYSIAN FIELDS.

What! you here? Why, old man, I never
Felt more surprise, or more delight.
Who would have dreamt that you would ever
Parade around in robes of white?
I always thought of you as dodging
The coals and fire-brands somewhere else;
And here you are, with board and lodging,
Where not so much as butter melts.

Well, well, old man, if you can stand it
Up here, I 'll never make a fuss.
I had forebodings that they 'd planned it
A little stiff for men like us.
The boys were much cut up about you,
You got away so very quick;
And as for me, to do without you —
It absolutely made me sick.

I wish you could have seen us plant you,
Why, every man squeezed out a tear.
And just imagine us, — now can't you? —
The gang, and yours the only bier!
Fred hammered out some bully verses;
We had them printed in the sheet,
With lines funereal as hearses
Around them. Oh, it did look sweet!

Halloo! Is that Sir Walter Raleigh?
I wish you 'd point the people out:
I want to look at Tom Macaulay;
Is Makepeace anywhere about?
Where 's Socrates? Where 's Sydney Carton?—
Oh, — I forgot: he was a myth.
If there 's a thing I 've set my heart on,
It is to play with Sydney Smith.

What? Glad I came? I am, for certain;
The other 's a malarious hole;

I always pined to draw the curtain,
And, somehow, knew I had a soul.
The flesh, — oh, was n't it a fetter?
You 'd get so tired of all your schemes.
But here I think I 'll like it better;
Oh dear, how natural it seems!

4

A SECOND THOUGHT.

This world's the worst I ever saw;
I'd like to make it better.
I'm going to promulgate the law,
And hold men to its letter.
> Be respectable, and stand
> Esteemed of Mrs. Grundy;
> Attend to business week-days, and
> Read moral books on Sunday.

On Sabbath-keepers, every one,
Approvingly I smile, and
Frown on those who spend their Sun-
Days down at Coney Island.
> Don't play cards, young man; Gobang
> Affords amusement ample.
> Speak carefully, eschewing slang,
> And set a good example.

The theatres, — how bad they be!
The players, — oh, how vicious!
The waltz I shudder when I see,
And think it most pernicious.

    Shun the wine-cup: don't be led
    To drink by scoff or banter;
    In the cup lurk pains of head,
    And snakes in the decanter.

    ·   ·   ·   ·   ·   ·

Ah me! I wonder if I 'm right!
I say it 's wrong to do so,
As though, without a soul in sight,
I ruled alone, like Crusoe.

    Is it that I am partly wrong,
    And partly right, my neighbor,
  -And that we get, who toil so long,
    Half truths for all our labor?

A PRACTICAL QUESTION.

DARKLY the humorist
Muses on fate;
Ghastly experiment
Life seems to him;
Subject for merriment
Sombre and grim.
Is it his doom, or is 't
Something he ate?

ET TU, BERGHE!

AND art thou, Bergh, so firmly set
Against domestic strife
As to correct with stripes the man
Who disciplines his wife?

Such action does not of thy creed
Appear the normal fruit:
Thou shouldst befriend a being who
Behaves so like a brute!

INSOMNIA.

Come, vagrant sleep, and close the lid
Upon the casket of my thought!
Come, truant, come when thou art bid,
And let thyself be caught!

For lonely is the night, and still,
And, save my own, no breath I hear;
No other mind, no other will,
Nor heart, nor hand, is near.

Thy waywardness what prayer can move?
Canst thou by any lure be brought?

Or art thou, then, like woman's love,
That only comes unsought?

Up! Where 's my dressing - gown? My pipe is
here.

Slumber be hanged! Now for a book and beer.

CIVIL SERVICE.

On Pennsylvania Avenue
He stood and waited for a car;
He turned to catch a parting view
Of where the Public Buildings are.
He looked at them with thoughtful eye;
He took his hat from off his head;
He heaved a half-regretful sigh,
And thus he said:

" My relative, I do the bidding
Of Fate, and say to thee good-by.
I think thee fortunate at ridding
Thyself of such a clerk as I.
Thy sure support, though somewhat meagre,
Hath much about it to commend;
Nor am I now so passing eager
To leave so provident a friend.

" Light was thy yoke, could I have borne it
  With tranquil mind and step sedate :
  Why did my feeble shoulders scorn it,
  And seem to crave a heavier weight?
  Extremely blest is his condition
  Whose needs thy bounteous hands supply,
  If he but fling away ambition,
  And let the world go rushing by.

" *Indocilis pauperiem pati,*
  I must get out of this damp spot.
  Away! away! Whatever fate I
  May have in store, I fear it not.
  Away from all my soul despises,
  From paltry aims, from sordid cares ;
  Fame, honor, love, time's richest prizes,
  Lie waiting for the man who dares.

" The man who calls no man his master,
  Nor bows his head to tinsel gods;

Who faces debt, disease, disaster,
And never murmurs at the odds,
Although his life from its beginning
Marks only fall succeeding fall, —
Let him fight on, and trust to winning
In death the richest prize of all."

He jammed his hat down on his head;
He turned from where the Buildings are;
Precipitately thence he fled,
And caught a passing car.

ALL OR NOTHING.

Happy the man whose far remove
From business and the giddy throng
Fits him in the paternal groove
Unquestioning to glide along;
Apart from struggle and from strife,
Content to live by labor's fruits,
And wander down the vale of life
In gingham shirt and cowhide boots.

He too is blest who, from within
By strong and lasting impulse stirred,
Faces the turmoil and the din
Of rushing life; whom hope deferred
But more incites; who ever strives,
And wants, and works, and waits, until
The multitude of other lives
Pay glorious tribute to his will.

But he who, greedy of renown,
Is too tenacious of his ease, —
Alas for him! Nor busy town
Nor country with his mood agrees.
Eager to reap, but loath to sow,
He longs *monstrari digito;*
And looking on with envious eyes,
Lives restless, and. obscurely dies.

A PHILADELPHIA CLAVERHOUSE.

To the fathers in council 't was Witherspoon spoke :
"Our best beloved dogmas we cannot revoke.
God's infinite mercy let others record,
And teach men to trust in their crucified Lord;
The old superstitions let others dispel;
I feel it my duty to go in for hell.

" Perdition is needful; beyond any doubt
Hell fire is a thing that we can't do without.
The bottomless pit is our very best claim;
To leave it unworked were a sin and a shame:
We must keep it up, if we like it, or not,
And make it eternal, and make it red hot.

" To others the doctrine of love may be dear;
I own I confide in the doctrine of fear:

There's nothing, I think, so effective to make
Our weak fellow-creatures their errors forsake,
As to tell them abruptly, with unchanging front,
'You'll be damned if you do! You'll be damned
    if you don't!'

"Saltpetre and pitchforks, with brimstone and coals
Are arguments suited to rescue men's souls.
A new generation forthwith must arise,
With Beelzebub pictured before their young eyes:
They'll be brave, they'll be true, they'll be
    gentle and kind,
Because they have Satan forever in mind."

THROWING STONES.

"I LOVE my child," the actress wrote.
"My duty is to guide
  The child I bore, and in my arms
  The child I love shall hide: · `
  Shall hide from missiles cast at me,
  Because I have so odd
  A conscience that I choose to rear
  The child I took from God."

  There is a sin from which us all
  May gracious Heaven guard;
  Which is its own worst punishment,
  Itself its sole reward.
  And of it social law has said
  To man, "If sin you must,

Go, then! And come again, but leave
The woman in the dust!"

Ah! who can know, save Him Allwise
Who watches from above,
The awful hazard women dare
To run for men they love?
Or tell how many a craven heart,
To shield his own bad name,
Has caused a woman's trustful love
To bring her lasting shame?

To her who, when the dream has passed,
Finds herself left alone,
And in her crushed, repentant heart
A yearning to atone,
Heaven, more merciful than man,
Who erst upon her smiled,
By love to win her to itself
May send a little child.

Then, if the lonely mother's heart
Accepts the gracious gift,
And if the charge she dared to take
She does not dare to shift;
Shall we, untempted and untried,
To ease and virtue born,
Visit upon her shrinking head
Our unrelenting scorn?

We, who have all our lives been taught
Truths other men have learned,
And walked by what celestial light
In other bosoms burned;
We, whose sublimest duty is
To do as we are bid, —
How shall we judge a soul from which
The face of God is hid?

Know you the loneliness of heart
That courts release from Death?

That makes it burdensome to draw
Each slow, successive breath?
That longs for human sympathy,
Until, when hope is lost,
A respite from its agony
It buys at any cost?

Of erring human nature we
Are born each with his share:
We all are vain; we all are weak,
And quick to fly from care;
And if we keep our footing,
Or seem to rise at all,
'T were well for us with charity
To look on those who fall.

And if our hands are strengthened,
And if our lips can speak,
'T were well if with them we might help
Our brothers who are weak;

And well if we remember
God's love is never grudged,
And never sit in judgment,
If we would not be judged.

TOUCHING BOTTOM.

THINK that I have somewhere read
About a man, whose foolish head,
By mischievous intention led,
      A sprite
Had with an ass's visage decked,
That all who met him might detect
His intellectual defect
      At sight.

The trite remark of man and book,
That many men are men in look,
But donkeys really, thus the spook

           Reversed.

The victim of the imp's·design
Had such a head as yours or mine,
Although his did look asinine

           At first.

But Love — I think the story ran —
Was proof against the fairy's plan,
Discerning, through the mask, the man,

           Perhaps;

Or is it true that women try
But very faintly to descry
Long ears on heads that occupy

           Their laps?

I know a youth whose fancy gropes
For head-gear finer than the Pope's;

So him his bright and treacherous hopes
                    Delude.
But in the mirror of his fears
When this too sanguine person peers,
Alas! behold the jackass ears
                    'Protrude!

To him it happens, now and then,
That over products of his pen
He cackles, as o'er eggs the hen
                    Who lays,
To find that to another's ear
His cherished sentiments appear,
Not utterances strong and clear,
                    But brays.

Titania mine, if I could find
You ever to my follies blind,
Such deep content would rule my mind
                    Within

That, even though myself aware
Of pointed ears adorned with hair,
I do not think that I should care
    A pin.

HONI SOIT QUI MAL Y PENSE.

IT was my happy lot to meet,
Upon a late occasion,
While seeking of the summer's heat
Agreeable evasion,
By visiting at a resort
Of fashion, — where, no matter, —
A maid whom there was none to court,
And very few to flatter.

Her head had not the graceful poise
Of Aphrodite's statue;
Her hair reminded you of boys,
Her nose was pointed at you.
A Derby hat, the self-same sort
The fashionable male owes
Money for, she used to sport,
As angels do their haloes.

She seldom walked in silk attire,
But commonly in flannel;
Nor yet in oils did she aspire
To figure on a panel:
Because she could not help but see
She was not tall nor slender;
Nor did she deem her curves to be
Superlatively tender.

Some prudish dames did her abuse
With censure fierce and scathing,
Because she, happening to lose
Her stocking while in bathing,
Deemed such a loss of little note,
And made no fuss about it;
But tied the stocking round her throat,
And reappeared without it.

I do not think that for the pelf
Of eligible boobies,

Or for the chance to deck herself
With diamonds and rubies,
Or for her standing in the books
Of prim and proper ladies,
Or for their disapproving looks,
She cared a hoot from Hades.

Though competent to hold her tongue,
When circumstance demanded
Speech, she was, for one so young,
Astonishingly candid.
She sang the cheerfullest of songs,
Which, sung by her, were funny;
And never brooded on her wrongs,
Or hoarded up her money.

'T is true, this careless damsel's fame
At last grew rather shady,
But if the man disposed to name
Her fast, or not a lady,

Permits his strictures to be aired
Where I can overhaul him,
The present writer is prepared
To strict account to call him.

HIS WASHERWOMAN.

"My laundress! my laundress! she causes me dis-
    tress,
And woe, and anguish infinite, and endless bitter-
    ness."
'Twas thus, with fingers in his hair, exclaimed the
    Muse's scion,

And gazed upon — the night was fair — Arcturus
    and Orion.

" Her bill she has sent in to me. What shall my
    cares dispel?

For how to pay that small account I cannot, can-
    not tell!

" My laundress! my laundress! When first for me
    she washed,

My brow was smooth, my eye was clear, my soul
    was unabashed ;

And when she came to get my clothes my manner
    was urbane,

And I looked up and smiled, and asked if it were
    going to rain ;

And she with all humility her eyes to mine would
    raise,

Then, glancing at the clouds, would murmur, ' Yes,
    sor, av ye plaze !'

"My laundress! my laundress! Her ways are al-
  tered now,
And when she comes for clothes she comes with
  scorn upon her brow;
With eyes downcast upon my book, I sit absorbed
  and still,
Until she says, 'Young man, I'd loike the money
  fur me bill:
Me childer has no shoes to wear, me rint is overdue.
Pay up, young man, and I'll not be a troublin' of
  you!'

"My laundress! my laundress! She sends a shad-
  owy boy
To watch me mornings while I sleep, and damp my
  rising joy;
And when I wake from tranquil dreams and inno-
  cent repose,
That small gossoon beside my bed is sitting on my
  clothes.

He only says 'Miss Grady 'd loike the money, sor,
    to-day.'
I, speechless, turn toward the wall; he, silent, goes
    away.

"I 'll go and see my laundress, and speak the
    truth unmasked;
I 'll tell her how impossible a favor she has asked;
I 'll say that I am penniless, and if I put up spout
As much of my effects as I could get along with-
    out,   ·
The sum that I would realize upon them would
    amount
To only one poor third of what is due on her ac-
    count.

"I 'll say I sometimes contemplate absconding from
    the place,
But that I 'm not a scoundrel scamp, like Thack-
    eray's Deuceace;

And though I cannot pay her bill, I will not run
    away;
And then I 'll listen patiently to what she has to
    say.
And when vituperation has taken off the edge
Of her just wrath, I 'll speak, and thus I 'll put
    myself in pledge.

" I 'll say, ' You have a daughter; I know she is not
    fair,
But never for mere looks did I particularly care.
I often have remarked her, as, when the day was
    fine,
She went with sprightly grace to hang my clothes
    upon the line;
And oft have I addressed her, and, though her
    speech was curt,
I learned to love her, as she fixed a clothespin on
    my shirt!

" ' I 'll cultivate your daughter ; I 'll woo her with
an art

That shall not fail to quickly make impression on
her heart;

And when her young affections with subtlety I 've
won,

I trust that you, dear madam, will receive me as
your son.

The duties that devolve on me I 'll never try to
shirk,

And what I cannot pay in cash you shall receive
in work.' "

THE END